Nā

____

tēnei pukapuka

This book belongs to

____

Completed during a Wild Creations residency in Karamea, 2007.
The author gratefully acknowledges the support of
Creative New Zealand and the Department of Conservation.

Dedicated to the children of Mapua School.

PUFFIN BOOKS
Published by the Penguin Group
Penguin Group (NZ), 67 Apollo Drive, Rosedale,
North Shore 0632, New Zealand (a division of Pearson New Zealand Ltd)
Penguin Group (USA) Inc., 375 Hudson Street, New York, New York 10014, USA
Penguin Group (Canada), 90 Eglinton Avenue East, Suite 700, Toronto,
Ontario, M4P 2Y3, Canada (a division of Pearson Penguin Canada Inc.)
Penguin Books Ltd, 80 Strand, London, WC2R 0RL, England
Penguin Ireland, 25 St Stephen's Green,
Dublin 2, Ireland (a division of Penguin Books Ltd)
Penguin Group (Australia), 250 Camberwell Road, Camberwell,
Victoria 3124, Australia (a division of Pearson Australia Group Pty Ltd)
Penguin Books India Pvt Ltd, 11, Community Centre,
Panchsheel Park, New Delhi – 110 017, India
Penguin Books (South Africa) (Pty) Ltd, 24 Sturdee Avenue,
Rosebank, Johannesburg 2196, South Africa

Penguin Books Ltd, Registered Offices: 80 Strand, London, WC2R 0RL, England

First published by Puffin Books, 2008
20 19 18 17 16 15

Designed by Cheryl Rowe
Prepress by Image Centre Limited
Printed in China through Asia Pacific Offset

ISBN 9780143502838

A catalogue record for this book is available
from the National Library of New Zealand.

www.penguin.co.nz

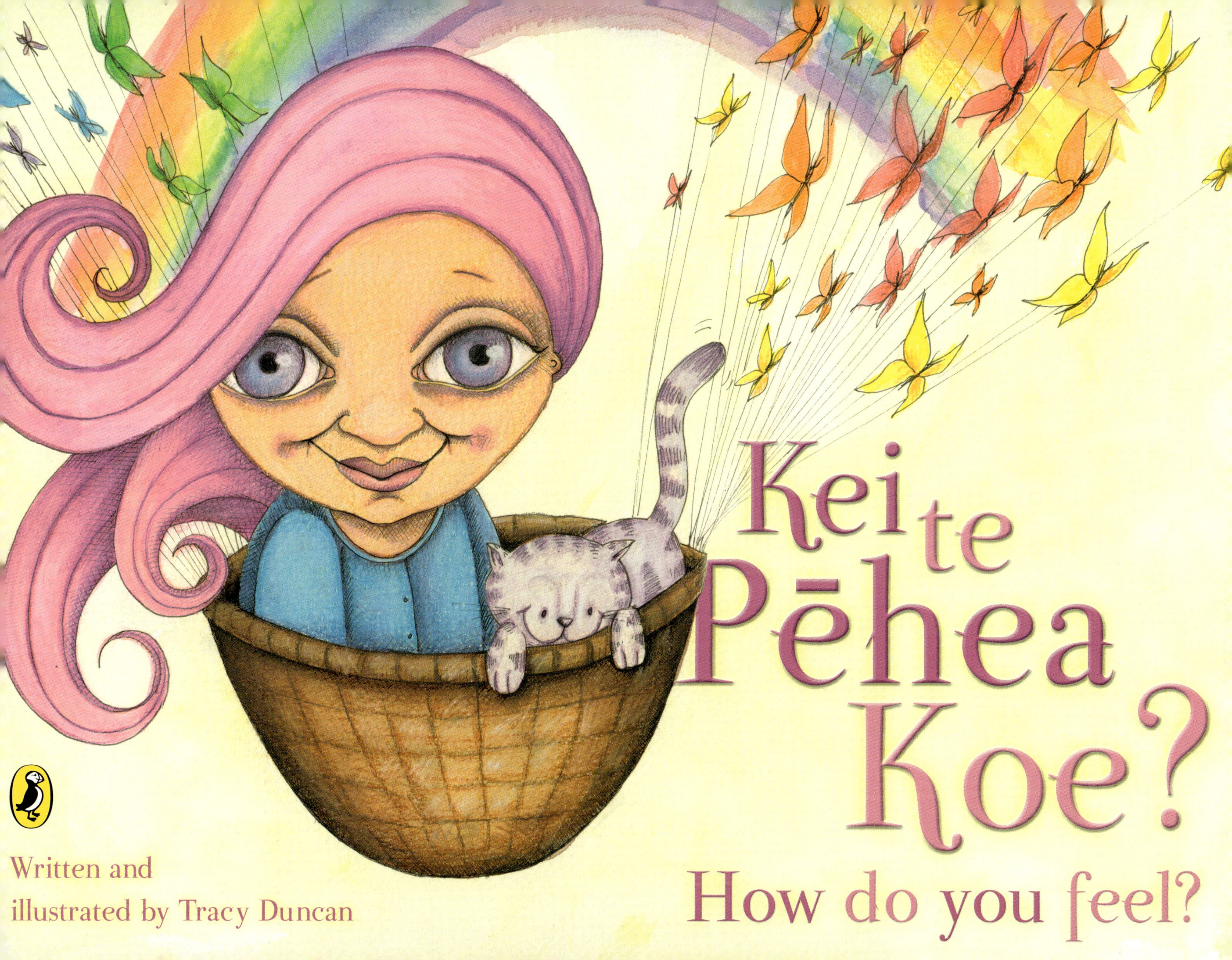
Kei te Pēhea Koe?
How do you feel?
Written and
illustrated by Tracy Duncan

Kei te pēhea koe?

How do you feel?

Kei te makariri au

I feel cold

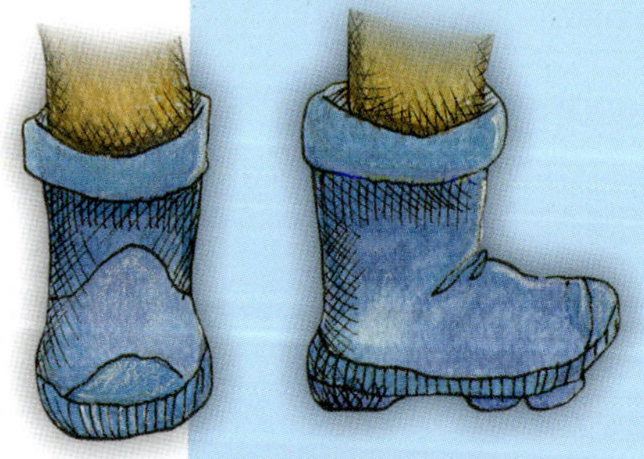

Kei te wera au

I feel hot

Kei te mokemoke au

I feel lonely

Kei te matekai au

I feel hungry

Kei te ngenge au

I feel tired

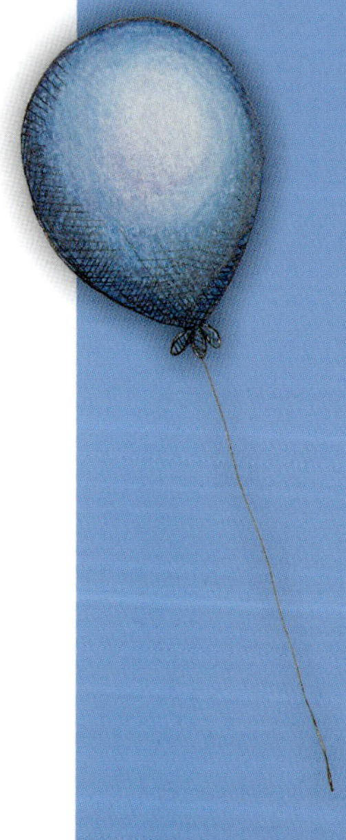

Kei te mataku au

I feel scared

Kei te pukuriri au

I feel angry

Kei te pūhaehae au

I feel jealous

Kei te pōuri au

I feel sad

Kei te whakamā au

I feel shy

Kei te pēhea koe?

How do you feel?

Kei te pai rawa au!

I feel fantastic!

How to pronounce Te Reo Māori

First of all, don't be scared! Have a go! It can seem tricky at first but, like everything, it gets easier with practice. Ask a friend for help if you get stuck.

Remember, Māori vowels sound different to English vowel sounds. Use this as a guide to help you pronounce the words in this book.

A = is pronounced ah, as in are
E = is pronounced eh, as in egg
I = is pronounced ee, as in see
O = is pronounced or, as in or
U = is pronounced oo, as in moon

For example, Kei te pēhea koe?
is Kay teh (as in te ar) peh (is in pe ar)
– he-ah ko (as in or) – eh?

Kei te ngenge is the trickiest
to pronounce.
Say the ng (as in si ng) and it sounds
close to kay teh ng-eh ng-eh.

Have fun and good luck!

Kei te pēhea koe?

About the author

Born in Mangakino and raised on the Coromandel Peninsula, Tracy Duncan now lives in the Moutere Hills of Nelson, where she shares her orchard home with her husband, two children and an ever-growing variety of furred and feathered critters.

Her paintings are represented by a variety of galleries throughout New Zealand. She is a participant in the NZ Book Council's *Writers in Schools* program, and in 2007 was awarded a Creative New Zealand/DOC *Wild Creations* artists' residency, which saw her spend six productive weeks in Karamea, on the West Coast of the South Island.

For more details, check out her website on www.tracyduncan.co.nz